Old MacDonald Had a Farm

Library of Congress Cataloging-in-Publication Data

Old MacDonald had a farm.

Summary: The inhabitants of Old MacDonald's farm are
described, verse by verse.
1. Folk-songs, English—United States. [1. Folk
songs, American] I. Rounds, Glen, 1906-   ill.
PZ8.3.0422 1989   784.4'05   88-24640

ISBN 0-8234-0739-X

Old MacDonald
Had a Farm

illustrated by
Glen Rounds

Holiday House/New York

COW

Old MacDonald had a farm,
EE-AY, EE-AY, OH!

And on that farm he had some

COWS,

EE-AY, EE-AY, OH!

With a MOO-MOO here,
And a MOO-MOO there,
Here a MOO, there a MOO,
Everywhere a MOO-MOO!

PIG

Old MacDonald had a farm,
EE-AY, EE-AY, OH!

And on that farm he had some

PIGS,

EE-AY, EE-AY, OH!

With an OINK-OINK here,
And an OINK-OINK there,
Here an OINK, there an OINK,
Everywhere an OINK-OINK!

ROOSTER

Old MacDonald had a farm,
EE-AY, EE-AY, OH!

And on that farm he had some

ROOSTERS,

EE-AY, EE-AY, OH!

With a COCK-A-DOODLE here,
And a COCK-A-DOODLE there,
Here a DOODLE, there a DOODLE,
Everywhere a COCK-A-DOODLE!

SHEEP

Old MacDonald had a farm,
EE-AY, EE-AY, OH!

And on that farm he had some

SHEEP,

EE-AY, EE-AY, OH!

With a BAA-BAA here,
And a BAA-BAA there,
Here a BAA, there a BAA,
Everywhere a BAA-BAA!

DOG

Old MacDonald had a farm,
EE-AY, EE-AY, OH!

And on that farm he had some

DOGS,

EE-AY, EE-AY, OH!

With a BOW-WOW here,
And a BOW-WOW there,
Here a BOW-WOW, there a BOW-WOW,
Everywhere a BOW-WOW!

TURKEY

Old MacDonald had a farm,
EE-AY, EE-AY, OH!

And on that farm he had some

TURKEYS,
EE-AY, EE-AY, OH!

With a GOBBLE-GOBBLE here,
And a GOBBLE-GOBBLE there,
Here a GOBBLE, there a GOBBLE,
Everywhere a GOBBLE-GOBBLE!

HORSE

Old MacDonald had a farm,
EE-AY, EE-AY, OH!

And on that farm he had a

HORSE,

EE-AY, EE-AY, OH!

With a NEIGH-NEIGH here,
And a NEIGH-NEIGH there,
Here a NEIGH, there a NEIGH,
Everywhere a NEIGH-NEIGH!

DUCK

Old MacDonald had a farm,
EE-AY, EE-AY, OH!

And on that farm he had some

DUCKS,

EE-AY, EE-AY, OH!

With a QUACK-QUACK here,
And a QUACK-QUACK there,
Here a QUACK, there a QUACK,
Everywhere a QUACK-QUACK!

CAT

Old MacDonald had a farm,
EE-AY, EE-AY, OH!

And on that farm he had some

CATS,

EE-AY, EE-AY, OH!

With a MEOW-MEOW here,
And a MEOW-MEOW there,
Here a MEOW, there a MEOW,
Everywhere a MEOW-MEOW!

HEN

Old MacDonald had a farm,
EE-AY, EE-AY, OH!

And on that farm he had some

HENS,

EE-AY, EE-AY, OH!

With a CLUCK-CLUCK here,
And a CLUCK-CLUCK there,
Here a CLUCK, there a CLUCK,
Everywhere a CLUCK-CLUCK!

CROW

Old MacDonald had a farm,
EE-AY, EE-AY, OH!

And on that farm he had some

CROWS,

EE-AY, EE-AY, OH!

With a CAW-CAW here,
And a CAW-CAW there,
Here a CAW, there a CAW,
Everywhere a CAW-CAW!

GOOSE

Old MacDonald had a farm,
EE-AY, EE-AY, OH!

And on that farm he had some

GEESE,

EE-AY, EE-AY, OH!

With a HONK-HONK here,
And a HONK-HONK there,
Here a HONK, there a HONK,
Everywhere a HONK-HONK!

GUINEA HEN

Old MacDonald had a farm,
EE-AY, EE-AY, OH!

And on that farm he had some

GUINEA HENS,

EE-AY, EE-AY, OH!

With a POT-RACK here,
And a POT-RACK there,
Here a POT-RACK, there a POT-RACK,
Everywhere a POT-RACK!

SKUNK

Old MacDonald had a farm,
EE-AY, EE-AY, OH!

And on that farm he had a

SKUNK,
EE-AY, EE-AY, OH!

With a PEE-YOO here,
And a PEE-YOO there,
Here a PEE-YOO, there a PEE-YOO,
Everywhere a PEE-YOO!

Old MacDonald had a farm,